BRITNEY MAKES A BUDGET

Madelyn McManus

ROSEN
COMMON CORE
READERS

Rosen
Classroom™

New York

Published in 2014 by The Rosen Publishing Group, Inc.
29 East 21st Street, New York, NY 10010

Book Design: Mickey Harmon

Photo Credits: Cover, p. 7 (girl) Juriah Mosin/Shutterstock.com; pp. 2–24 (background) Natali Glado/Shutterstock.com;
p. 5 (calculator) docent/Shutterstock.com; p. 9 (paper) Stephen Rees/Shutterstock.com; p. 9 (wood grain) Minerva Studio/
Shutterstock.com; p. 13 (checkout) Tyler Olson/Shutterstock.com; p. 15 (theater) Hermera/Thinkstock.com; p. 17 (piggy
bank) Jason Stitt/Shutterstock.com; p. 19 (bank) Frontpage/Shutterstock.com; p. 21 (vet) Gelpi/Shutterstock.com.

ISBN: 978-1-4777-2528-3
6-pack ISBN: 978-1-4777-2529-0

Manufactured in the United States of America

CPSIA Compliance Information: Batch #CS13RC: For further information contact Rosen Publishing, New York, New York at 1-800-237-9932.

CONTENTS

THE FAMILY BUDGET

Britney's parents make a budget every month. A budget tells you how to spend your money and how to save it. Britney's dad says budgeting is important because it helps you spend your money wisely.

Britney is helping her parents make the budget this month. Learning how to budget will teach Britney how to handle her money when she's older!

What sort of things do you think should be in a family's budget?

4

5

Before they begin, Britney's parents teach her how a budget works. Her parents explain that you have to earn money before you can buy things.

Britney's parents earn money by having jobs. They work hard to give their family what they need. Britney earns money, too. She gets an allowance for doing chores and helping around the house.

An allowance is money you can earn by doing chores or helping your parents.

THREE COLUMNS

Britney's mom says the first step in making a budget is knowing how much money you have. All the money you spend or save is based on that number.

Britney's mom divides a sheet of paper into three **columns**: "spend," "save," and "give." The first column is for money that's used right away. The second column is for having money in the future. The third column is for money used to help others.

Every family's budget is different! The amount of money that goes to each column depends on what a family decides.

▶

spend	save	give

THE SPEND COLUMN

Britney's dad says the "spend" column should always come first. That way, you know there's enough money to pay for everything you need.

Britney makes a list of her family's bills. It includes money used for expenses, such as their house and car, food, clothing, and spending money. Spending money is used for fun things, like going to the movies.

There are many expenses a family can spend money on.
Can you think of some?

WHERE DOES THE MONEY GO?

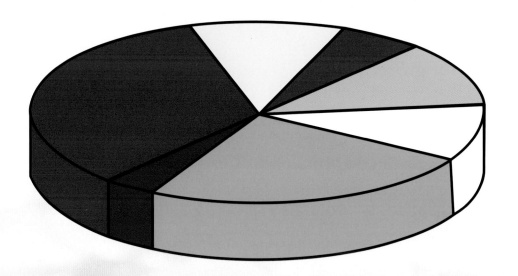

■	house expenses	■	food
■	car expenses	□	clothes
□	bills	■	spending money
		■	other

Britney's mom says that even though they have enough money, it's important to use it smartly. That's part of making a good budget!

For example, Britney's family budgets a certain amount of money for groceries. They want to get what they need without spending too much. When Britney's mom goes grocery shopping, she uses **coupons** and buys what's on sale. This lets her buy a lot of food while also sticking to the budget.

Buying things on sale or with coupons helps you get as much as you can with the money you've budgeted.

13

Britney's family has a lot of expenses, but her dad says it's important to spend money on fun things, too. However, their spending money is only a small part of the budget. There are many other things their money must be used for.

Britney's dad explains that budgeting is about making choices. Even though it would be fun to spend their extra money on toys, movies, or pizza, Britney knows they must use most of their money to pay bills.

Britney's family does one fun activity a week. They have to choose what they want to do the most, since they can't do everything!

THE SAVE COLUMN

Most of the money that's left after expenses goes in the "save" column. Saving is important because it gives you money for the future and for unexpected expenses, such as when something breaks and needs to be fixed.

Money can also be put in the "save" column to buy things you can't afford right away. Britney wants to buy a video game, but it's **expensive**! She saves for it by putting a little bit of her allowance in her piggy bank each week.

Putting money away week by week can add up to a lot!

Britney's parents save as much money as they can. Last year, her mom's car broke down. It was expensive to fix. Luckily, her family had enough in their savings account to cover it.

Britney's parents also save money so Britney and her sister can go to **college** one day. They began saving when Britney was young, because it takes a long time to save a lot of money!

A savings account is a special bank account. People put money in a savings account to keep it separate from the rest of their money.

19

THE GIVE COLUMN

The last column in Britney's family budget is the "give" column. Britney's dad says it's important to do good things for other people and for our world. One way to do this is to put money aside for **charities** or other good causes.

Britney's family loves animals, so they **donate** some of their money to the local animal shelter. This money helps make sure the animals have enough food, water, and care.

Many charities don't make enough money to cover their expenses. They rely on donations to get the money they need.

FINISHING THE BUDGET

Britney learns that it takes a lot of hard work to make a budget. Sometimes it's even harder to stick to it! But it's one of the most important things you can do. Budgeting your money shows you're **responsible**.

Britney will use the tools she learned from making her family's budget to spend and save her allowance wisely. Do you budget your allowance? What do you spend it on?

GLOSSARY

charity (CHEHR-uh-tee) A group that helps those in need or works for a good cause.

college (KAH-lihj) A school you attend after high school.

column (KAH-luhm) One part of a page that has been separated from top to bottom.

coupon (KOO-pahn) A piece of paper that's used to get money off something you buy at the store.

donate (DOH-nayt) To give away freely.

expensive (ihk-SPEHN-sihv) Costing a lot of money.

responsible (rih-SPAHN-suh-buhl) Able to choose for oneself what is right.

INDEX